1

Jack woke with a start. He stared out the windshield. *Where ...? Oh, yeah*, he thought when his gaze fell on the rest stop's restroom at the top of the hill. He checked the time: a quarter past four. *Sun should be up soon.* A rumble pulled his attention to the rearview mirror, and he watched an old, rusty Chevy pickup slowly drive through the parking lot.

A light flared in the cab, and for a split second, he could see the man holding the lit match. Everything about him seemed stretched, and he was so thin, Jack wondered if he was just skin and bones. He wore a camouflage trucker's cap, and wisps of dirty blond hair stuck out by his ears. The flame went out, leaving only the glowing red end of a cigarette visible.

Unease settled over Jack, and he shifted so he could keep his eyes locked on the truck as it continued forward at a snail's pace. Just before the road forced them back onto the highway, the truck turned right and disappeared into the surrounding woods.

"Huh," he mumbled through a yawn. He ran his hands over his face.

"What was that?" Sara asked from the back seat, leaning forward to poke her head between the front seats.

"Jesus, warn me next time," he grumbled, glancing over to see if they woke up her sister. "Now be quiet; Kylie is still asleep."

"No, I'm not," she replied before sitting up to stretch. "That truck was loud."

"Almost as loud as Uncle Jack's snoring," Sara said with a giggle.

THE REST STOP

BY
ERIC BUTLER

Naked Cat Press

The Rest Stop

Copyright © 2023 by Eric Butler.

For information contact:
Naked Cat Press
http://www.nakedcatpress.com
edbutler17@gmail.com

Paperback ISBN : 9798862493733

Book design by Naked Cat Press
Cover design by Grim Poppy Design
Edited by Lisa Lee
First Edition : September 2023
10 9 8 7 6 5 4 3 2 1

TO

ANGELIQUE,
I HOPE YOUR
BIRTHDAY
WAS A BLAST.

"Or your farting," Kylie said through her yawn.

"Yeah, and you can't taste my snores," Jack said with a side-eyed glance to the backseat.

Sara's eyes grew wide, and she slapped his shoulder. "Don't be gross, Uncle Jack."

Laughing, he leaned away enough to lessen the force of each strike. "Okay, okay. I give up. They don't taste like anything … But the smell … Woo-wee."

Sara squealed and increased her attack. Jack threw up his hands in surrender, and his laughter joined Kylie's. Sara slumped back and crossed her arms with a huff.

"Well, since we're all up, how about we take care of business and then hit the road?"

"Can we stop at Dunkin?"

"Sure, I need some coffee if I'm going to stay awake. All this driving is exhausting," he said, glancing at Kylie. "I don't know how I let your mom talk me into driving y'all to the new house."

"Somebody had to do it," Sara said, motioning to her sister. "I'm too young, and Kylie won't get behind the wheel since ... well, you know."

A silence fell over the car, and Kylie got out. She pushed the door closed harder than necessary, and Sara flinched.

"You know better," Jack said with a shake of his head. He slipped out of the car.

Kylie stood on the sidewalk, her back to the vehicle. Jack moved to the trunk and popped it open. He grabbed the two travel bags sitting next to the suitcases and softly closed the trunk. She glanced back and watched him walk towards her on the car's passenger side.

"You know she didn't mean anything by that," he said, holding out his arms.

"I know." she said with a nod, and stepped into his hug, burying her face against his chest. She took a deep, shuddered breath.

The back door opened, and Sara called out, "Sorry." Jack pulled back his left arm and motioned her in. She wrapped her arms around them and joined the hug.

"It's okay," Kylie mumbled into his shirt and pulled back.

He held out the girls' bag and pointed to the restroom at the top of the hill. "The quicker we do this, the quicker we can get those donuts."

Jack let the sisters move ahead and glanced around, counting three other parked vehicles. He noticed two had orange tags on their windshields, and in the third, he realized a woman was watching them. Resisting the urge to wave, he walked around the railing to access the stairs. He smiled at his nieces as they threw their heads back and blew out clouds of condensation.

He picked up his pace to catch up with the girls. At the top, they turned left to circle back around another metal railing to get to the main walkway. *Worse than an amusement park line,* he thought with a shake of his head. A semitruck fired up across the street, and he wondered how long it would be before the driver drove away.

"Lonely life," he mumbled to himself.

"What was that, Uncle Jack?" Sara asked.

"I was just thinking how lonely those truck drivers must be without someone to talk to, and how you'd make a killing as a travel companion since you never stop talking."

"They'd want a refund after her first fart," Kylie said with a snort.

"Whatever," she replied, ignoring her sister's laughter.

A chill ran down his back, and he threw his arm around Sara's shoulders for a quick hug. "Brr, let's get this done and get back to a heated car."

"I like the design of this one," Kylie said over her shoulder.

Jack nodded, appreciating the open design with a single walkway that ran between the two halves of the building. It continued through, and he suspected he might find a table or two on the backside that matched the ones he just passed. On the left was a door marked Women, and on the right one for the men. Each side had two matching vending machines: one with drinks and the other filled with snacks.

"Don't dawdle," he said as he pushed on the men's door and entered.

The bathroom was dark, and the door swung closed to cut off the artificial light from outside. A buzz sounded, and four panels of lights began to hum as they lit up. He stepped to the sink, placed down his bag, and moved to the urinals. He let out a sigh and started to pee. When he finished, he stepped back, and after a moment, the urinal flushed. He moved to the sink, washed his hands, and fished out his toothbrush. His head shot up when he heard a female scream. Movement caught his eye, and he watched the bathroom stall door swing open behind him.

"Looks like Jimbo jumped the gun," a gravelly voice said.

Jack recognized the camouflage hat just before the hammer crashed down on the back of his head.

2

Kylie leaned against the sink and tried to ignore the sounds of her sister peeing in the stall. She stared at her reflection, and for a moment, she was back at the accident, her face covered in blood. She reached up and touched the scar hidden under her hairline, and her throat tightened. *Poor Johnny*. She prayed that memory wasn't next and focused on taking deep, even breaths.

The toilet flushed, and Sara slid next to her. "You gonna puke?" she asked and turned on the water to wash her hands.

"Shut it," Kylie mumbled and let out a shuddered breath.

She straightened up and unzipped the travel bag to pull out two toothbrushes and a tube of toothpaste. Sara squirted some on her brush and motioned for her sister to hold out hers. Kylie slipped the glob of paste under the water, hoping that some might get knocked off. *Always uses half the tube*, she thought, grateful for the distraction.

Kylie stared blankly at the mirror and began to brush up and down. For a minute, the movement reflected in the mirror didn't register. She blinked, and her hand froze mid-stroke. The middle stall door was slowly opening, and through the crack, she could see a wide eye watching them. Her gaze shifted down, and in the reflection, she could now see dirt-encrusted work boots under the door. *Those weren't there a minute ago.* Her heart sped up, and she was surprised Sara didn't hear it slamming against her chest. She spat out the wad of foam in her mouth and spun around.

"What are you doing?" she asked loudly, trying to keep the shake from her voice.

Sara glanced at her and turned around to see what her sister was staring at. The stall door pulled back and revealed a large man. He stepped into the main part of the bathroom and let the door swing back into place. Kylie guessed he was around six-five and close to three hundred pounds, but he didn't seem fat, just huge.

"I said what are you doing?" she barked, unnerved by his wide-eyed stare and lopsided grin.

"Is something wrong with him?" Sara asked, gobs of foam spilling from her mouth as she spoke.

"I don't know, but you need to go get Uncle Jack," Kylie said, stepping between the mute giant and her sister. "NOW."

Sara gave a start, surprised at the sharpness in Kylie's voice, and slid behind her sister to make her way towards the door. The man stood still, but his eyes followed her, and he began to snicker.

"Y'all are pretty," he said, his voice pitched higher than Kylie expected. "I like pretty."

Sara froze for a second, glancing back at her sister. The man sprang forward, pawing at her with thick, meaty fingers. She screamed when his hand tightened into a fist around her arm. Kylie rushed at him, dropping her toothbrush on the restroom floor. She raked her left hand across his face and scratched at the hand holding her sister with the other. He howled in pain and jerked his head back to get away from her long fingernails. His grip relaxed, and Sara pulled free and rushed to the door.

"Don't stop," Kylie hollered. "Get Uncle Jack."

She watched Sara slip out and darted back. The man hunched over and pressed his palm against his cheek. She could see blood running down his face to drip onto the floor in thick, red drops. She resisted the urge to rush to the sink and wash out the skin caked beneath her nails.

"That hurt," he said, a quiver in his voice. "A lot."

"You better just get the fuck out of here," she yelled, pointing at the door. "You go now before my uncle gets here, or you'll be sorry."

The man shook his head. "I'm already sorry, but not as sorry as you're gonna be."

Roaring, he swung his arm at her, balling his hand into a fist and striking her on the side of the head. Kylie's head snapped to the side, and stars filled her vision. She stumbled back, her arms waving to help retain her balance. He drove his fist into her stomach and drove the air from her. She fell to her knees and wrapped her arms around her belly. Tears leaked from her eyes, and she struggled to catch her breath.

He wrapped his fingers into her hair and jerked her head back. "Momma says it's best not to spare the rod when folks act up." He punched her in the face, and Kylie's world went dark.

3

Sara ran across the walkway to the men's room. There weren't any more sounds coming from the ladies' room, and she prayed she got to Uncle Jack in time. She slammed into the door and stumbled into the room with a yelp.

"Uncle Jack, there's a weirdo in the ..." She trailed off, unable to process what was before her.

Her uncle lay on the floor, but where his head should have been, there was just a pile of bloody mush. A lanky man knelt beside his body, and he ran his tongue over the pulpy mess, stopping to slurp in thick wads of gore. He leaned back and moaned; his eyes closed in ecstasy while he swallowed.

Sara screamed and jerked the door open to escape. The giant man stepped out of the women's restroom with Kylie slung over his shoulder like a ragdoll. He offered a smile, and blood ran down from the scratches on his cheek. Sara took another breath and released another scream. She turned and ran, heading towards the parking lot and her uncle's car.

"Look at her run," the giant man hollered out with a snort. "You better get a move on, Skeeter. She's gettin' away."

Sara glanced back and saw the lanky man start to give chase. She increased her speed, willing her legs to move faster, and swung her head forward just as she came upon the metal railing. She slammed into it with a grunt and ducked down to scurry through the bars. A whoosh of air stirred her hair, and fingertips swept down her back before she jerked away.

"Damn it," the man shouted. "Get back 'ere."

Sara scrambled forward, crawling on her hands and knees. She could see her uncle's car, and she prayed the spare keys were still in the glovebox. A few spots over, a car door opened, and she felt relief wash over her.

"Help. Help! Please, help me!" she screamed. Struggling to her feet, Sara rushed down the stairs. She resisted the urge to look back, terrified the man was gaining ground. Grabbing the rail, she began to take the steps two at a time, but her feet tangled up and she lost her grip. With a loud cry, she tumbled forward, bouncing off the steps until she rolled to a stop on the walkway.

"Hot damn," the lanky man hollered out. "Did you see that, Jimbo? She's a modern-day Mary Loo Retton."

She struggled to her hands and knees, using their harsh laughter as motivation.

"What's going on here?" a woman called out.

Sara slipped through the final railing and struggled to her feet. Her breath caught when her gaze fell on a woman standing by her car with the driver's side door open. *Almost there.* She lurched forward at the thought and began to wave at the woman.

"Start the car," she yelled between gasping breaths. "They're crazy."

The woman looked at her and then towards the rest stop building. She rushed over to the passenger door and opened it. "Hurry, they're right behind you."

Sara didn't think she could move any faster, between the aches and pain from the fall and the overwhelming helplessness of the situation sinking in. She just knew the lanky man would grab her any moment. Grab her and suck on her cuts and scrapes, the image of her uncle on the restroom floor suddenly all she could see.

"Almost there," the woman shouted.

Sara blinked away the memory and watched the woman scramble through the passenger's side and slide behind the wheel. The car's engine fired up, and Sara felt a surge of energy.

"God damn it," the man cried out, his voice sounding farther away than she could have hoped.

Sara dove into the seat and slammed the door shut, slamming her palm on the lock. She began to shake, and tears leaked from the corners of her eyes. She flinched when the woman put her hand on her shoulder, but after a moment, she lunged forward and wrapped her arms around the woman.

"Oh, thank you ... thank you," she murmured into the woman's chest.

"There, there," the woman said in a soothing, motherly voice. "It's gonna be all right. I promise you won't feel a thing."

Sara yelped at a sharp jab in her neck. There was a flush of warmth that quickly spread from the prick to envelop her entire body. She pulled back with a sway, suddenly unable to balance herself without effort. Her eyes slid from the smirking woman's face to the syringe she held up between them.

"I can't let those boys have all the fun.

4

The side of Kylie's face ached. She tried to focus on the pain, hoping it would pull her from her fog, but she continued to fade in and out. She thought she heard her sister scream, but that now seemed an eternity ago. *Where's Uncle Jack?* The question lingered in her head, but she pushed it away, suddenly aware she might not like the answer.

She groaned when the big man's hand dug into her side as he shifted her body on his shoulder.

"Hush now," he whispered. "Or she'll give you the sleeping juice too."

Kylie tried to focus on his words, but none of what he said made sense. Just as she started drifting back towards the darkness, a woman's voice pulled her back.

"Well, quit dawdling, Jimbo, and get these two down to the truck. And don't think for a moment I ain't tellin' your momma about the mess you made, Skeeter."

"She's your momma too, Mary Lou," the man replied with a huff. "I'll get it all cleaned up, but we really should pack up what's left of him for the dogs."

Jimbo tightened his grip on Kylie and dipped down. Her eyes fluttered open, and she watched him scoop Sara up and toss her listless body over his other shoulder. Her stomach lurched when he spun quickly and started to walk towards the back of the building. He stepped off the walkway and carefully worked his way down the incline towards the woods.

"Just get to the house," she called out. "I'll clean this up."

"Thank ya kindly," Skeeter called out. "Hold up, Jimbo, this guy weighs a ton."

Kylie's throat tightened. *This guy* could only mean one person. She scrunched her eyes tight, but her tears managed to leak out, catching in her eyelashes for a few seconds before dripping to the ground below. She squirmed, and Jimbo tightened his grip.

"You best behave," he said, digging his fingers into her side. "Or when we get home, Momma will tan your hide."

She let out a whimper and grew still. He relaxed his hold a bit and stepped past the artificial light and into the forest. Her stomach rolled at the herky-jerky movement Jimbo made as he picked his way through the undergrowth.

"God damn it," Skeeter said with a sigh. "We need to clear us a better path."

"Maybe don't kill them at the top of the hill," Jimbo offered. "Cuz a path would get attention, and Momma don't want that."

"True enough, but weren't no other way to deal with this motherfucker."

"So you keep saying," Jimbo replied. "Truck's just up ahead anyhow."

His steps evened out, and Kylie peeked open her eyes. They were on a strip of cleared forest ground just wide enough for people to walk single file through the trees. He sped up, and soon they were standing next to an old dark pickup truck. He shifted and dropped Sara into the bed with a thud.

"Don't get any ideas," he said with a hiss. "You won't be near as pretty if you keep making me hit you."

"What?" Skeeter called out.

Jimbo dropped Kylie into the bed and turned around. "Nothin', just ready to get home. Let me help you."

The truck bounced, and liquid splashed across Kylie's face. A hot, coppery scent filled her nose, and her stomach heaved. Vomit sprayed from her mouth. A large hand stroked her hair, and though she wanted to pull away, a part of her welcomed the comforting gesture. The truck's engine fired up with a low rumble, and Jimbo crawled into the back to sit with them. He settled his bulk with a deep sigh and reached out to pat Kylie on the back.

The truck rolled forward, gaining speed with each second. Jimbo leaned back and stared up through the break in the trees. He resumed stroking her hair, and she heard him say two words before the roar of the truck's engine drowned out the rest.

"So pretty."

5

The truck pulled to a stop, and Kylie heard the driver's door open, the squeal of unoiled hinges, and then the door slamming shut. The truck lurched forward a few feet and stopped again.

"Jimbo, get the gate," Skeeter called out.

The truck sank down and sprang back up with a shudder. Jimbo's boots hit the dirt, and he let out a grunt. She heard his heavy footsteps and then the unoiled hinges once again. She took a deep breath, gagging as the stench of death and vomit filled her nostrils. A soft moan came from Sara, and Kylie reached out until she found her sister's hand.

Skeeter began to laugh, and the truck pulled away, bouncing up and down on the uneven road. Jimbo cried out, but the words were lost in the roar of the engine.

"Sara?" she whispered, and then repeated her sister's name louder to be heard over the truck.

The truck sharply veered to the right, and Kylie slid to the left through the vomit. Unwilling to let go of her sister, she held up her free hand and cried out when it smooshed into what was left of her uncle's head. Bile rose up her throat, and she jerked her hand back when the vehicle straightened. Swallowing hard, she tried to wipe the sticky mess from her fingers on her sweatpants.

Headlights washed over the truck from behind, and a horn sounded. They drove a few more feet, and then the truck rolled to a stop. Two car doors opened and slammed shut.

"What's the big idea?" Jimbo yelled out, stomping towards the truck.

Skeeter cut the truck's engine and got out. "I was just funnin' with ya. Quit being such a crybaby. Besides, your giant ass could use the exercise."

"Any other time, I'd agree," Mary Lou said. "But not when we have company."

"Nothing happened."

Mary Lou peeked into the bed. Kylie squeezed her eyes tight and tried to stay motionless. "Yet, you moron. This one is playing possum. You're just lucky cleanin' up your mess didn't take too long. Let's get through the gate so y'all can get them into the stalls, and I'll go check on Momma."

Skeeter stalked over to a pedestrian gate and unlocked it. He pushed it open and kicked a rock in front of it to keep it open.

Mary Lou stomped by and motioned to the main gate. "Hurry up and get that open so Jimbo can get them closer to the barn."

Skeeter sighed and moved over to swing it open. Jimbo drove the truck through, and Skeeter locked up both gates while he parked between the house and the barn. Jimbo slid out and moved to the back. He reached down and grabbed Kylie by the arm, lifting her up until she had no choice but to let go of her sister. He slung her over his shoulder once again and clamped down on her backside to hold her in place. Her head spun as he swung around and stomped away from the truck.

"I guess I'll get the other one, yeesh," Skeeter barked out before mumbling to himself, "I got to do everything around here."

Jimbo didn't reply and continued towards the barn and the rising sun. Kylie twisted her head and tried to get a better look, but the sun blinded her at every angle.

"Quit squirmin'," he said, digging his fingers into her hip.

He stopped by a dark red door and reached out with his free hand to grab the lock, angling it so he could roll the combination with his thumb. *Three, eight, four, three.* Kylie repeated the number sequence a few more times until she was confident she wouldn't forget it. He pulled the lock free and swung the door open.

The barn was dimly lit, but she realized that was because there were only three rows of lights on. The main floor was open, and the space formed a T, with stables on one side of the aisle and a row of refrigeration units on the other. From the doorway, Kylie noticed what looked like two operating tables spaced out by the units. *What is this place?*

"Well, come on," Skeeter said from behind. "Let's drop them off, and then you can help me get the dogs fed."

Jimbo carried her to the first stall, opened the door, and laid her down on the hay covered floor. He stared at her for a moment, then shook his head and stepped back out. Skeeter studied him from the corner of his eyes and let out a long sigh before tossing Sara in. She landed with a groan, and Kylie wrapped her arms around the girl. She flinched when the door slammed shut and a lock clicked in place.

"Y'all behave, and maybe we'll remember to feed y'all," Skeeter said with a chuckle.

Their footsteps grew fainter and disappeared altogether after a moment. Kylie hugged her sister and began to rock back and forth.

"You poor thing," a woman whispered from the shadows. "He likes you."

6

"Who's there?" Kylie asked, staring into the dark corner of the stable.

"My name's Allison, and this is Ben," the woman said, crawling into the light with a young boy at her side. He clung to her side and watched Kylie with large, unblinking eyes. "Is she okay?"

"I think they gave her something," she answered, glancing down to watch the steady rise and fall of her sister's chest. "But, no … she's not okay. I mean how could we be?"

12

Kylie looked away and tried to blink away her sudden tears. There was no doubt in her mind her uncle was dead, and she was pretty sure they'd be joining him soon. She took a deep breath and glanced over at the woman. "Who are these people?"

"Lord only knows," she said with a shrug. Before she continued, she covered the boy's ears with her hands. "I think these people are harvesting organs and selling them."

"What?" Kylie hugged her sister tighter.

Allison glanced down, her eyes locked on the top of Ben's head. "I watched them cut up his father. They put the parts in those fridges. They drained him of all his blood and then fed the rest to their dogs."

"Jesus Christ," Kylie whispered.

Allison removed her hands and stroked Ben's hair. "Do you know what day it is …?" There was a pause, and Kylie realized she hadn't said their names yet.

"Kylie, my name is Kylie, and this is my sister, Sara. It's Wednesday."

"The fifteenth?"

She shook her head and swallowed before answering. "No. It's the twenty-second."

Allison gave a stiff nod. "They don't let sunlight in very often. It all blurs together."

A door swung open, and sunlight shined through the cracks in the stall's slats for a moment but disappeared when the door banged shut. A low hum sounded, and three banks of lights flickered on over the tables. Allison scooted back into the shadows with Ben. Kylie gently laid her sister on the hay and crawled over to press her eye against one of the gaps.

Jimbo and Skeeter tossed her uncle's body on the table farthest from the stalls and began to strip the body. They chucked his clothes into a pile, and once he was nude, Skeeter moved over to the cabinet between two of the refrigeration units. He swung open the doors and pulled out a boning hook and a meat cleaver. He reached over, grabbed an apron from a hook, and slipped it over his head. Jimbo wheeled over a three-tiered utility cart and placed a bus tub on each level.

"Bet I can get it in one blow," Skeeter said, jamming the hook into the cadaver's hand and pulling the arm out to the side. He raised the cleaver up high, and his tongue poked out of the corner of his mouth as he concentrated.

Kylie's throat tightened. She wanted to look away but kept watching. She refused to abandon her uncle, even if it was just his body. Skeeter swung the cleaver, and it sliced through the flesh before jamming into the shoulder joint.

Skeeter glared at Jimbo. "Not a God damned word," he hissed, wiggling the cleaver to get it free. He raised it up again and slammed the cleaver back down with the same result. "Well, shit." He pulled it free again and flashed a smile. "Third time's the charm."

Jimbo nodded and let out a whoop when the cleaver chopped through. Jimbo worked the arm free from the hook and placed it in the bottom tub. Skeeter moved to the other side and jabbed the hook into the body's other hand.

The door opened, and a woman stomped in. "That's going to have to wait."

"Ah, Mary Lou," Skeeter whined. "I was just getting started."

"I need y'all to get the new girls' blood types. We got a rush order, so hop to it."

Jimbo turned and looked at the stall. Kylie jerked back and scrambled to her sister's side. Footsteps echoed throughout the barn, and she began to tremble as they drew closer. The door swung open, and Jimbo stepped in. Skeeter leaned out from behind the bigger man and held out a syringe.

"Peek-a-boo," he said, with a toothy grin. "Who's ready to get poked?"

Kylie flinched, the ache in her face reminding her what would happen if she put up any struggle. She glanced at her sister, suddenly jealous that she was unconscious and unaware of all that was happening.

"I'll behave, but I can tell you our blood types. We're both B-negative."

"And I'm the Queen of England," the woman called out from the other side. "You'll excuse me for not taking your word. Skeeter, get the samples."

He offered a shrug and ran his tongue across his lips. "You heard her."

Skeeter squatted, grabbed her wrist, and twisted her arm to expose the elbow pit. He jerked her forward and jabbed the needle into her skin. He got his sample and, after removing the needle, pressed his lips to the wound and sucked. He let out a soft moan, and his eyes closed to slits.

"That's enough, Skeeter," Jimbo grumbled, shifting his feet in frustration.

"Just a moment more," he mumbled against her flesh, and held out the needle for Jimbo to take.

Kylie tried to pull away, but Skeeter's grip tightened, and he sucked harder. She stared at the open door and wondered if she might be fast enough to get by. She was confident they weren't going to last much longer if she didn't get help. Her eyes darted to the syringe, and time seemed to slow. She lurched up, snatched the outstretched syringe, and jammed it towards Skeeter's eye socket. He flung his head back with a squeal and loosened his grip. She took one step, but Jimbo reached out quickly and wrapped his meaty hand around her throat. He lifted her off her feet and squeezed until her eyes bulged. She clawed at his hand, desperate to get a breath.

"Shouldn'ta done that," he said with a sigh. "Momma's not gonna be happy."

7

Ice cold water pulled Kylie from unconsciousness. She yelped in surprise, then sputtered when more splashed against her face.

"That's enough," a woman said, her voice raspy and deep.

Kylie saw three shapes through the watery haze and discovered when she moved to wipe her eyes that her hands were bound at the wrists and secured above her head. Her shoulders ached, and she realized she was not standing on the ground but dangled a foot or so above it. She blinked through the blur, and an old woman came into focus before her.

Skeeter stepped back with a bucket dangling from his left hand and a makeshift bandage covering his left eye. He sneered at her and let the bucket fall to the ground with a clatter. A match flaring pulled her attention back to the woman, who held the flame against the end of the cigarette dangling from her lips. She tossed the match, and it landed with a hiss in the puddle of water between them. She took a long drag until the tip blazed red.

"You got spirit, girl. I'll give you that. Might be what Jimbo is so infatuated with, though I suspect it's most likely your pretty face. He's not bright enough to realize beauty fades with time, and if you keep this up, I just might be persuaded to hasten the process," she said, blowing out a cloud of smoke in Kylie's direction. "You're just lucky that you missed doing Skeeter any permanent damage, and you helped teach him a valuable lesson."

Kylie wanted to shout at the woman, to demand they be let go, but an icy ball of fear was growing in her belly. "Where's my sister? Where's Sara?" she asked, her voice cracking with emotion.

The woman blew another cloud of smoke in Kylie's direction. "Oh, she's not far away. Mary Lou's getting her ready." She motioned back with her head towards the tables and a lady wearing scrubs.

Uncle Jack was gone, but evidence of his innards lay smeared on the tabletop and the barn floor. On the other table, Sara lay still. Mary Lou secured her to the table with Velcro straps around her wrists and ankles and moved over to the cabinets.

"You see, I figure direct punishment won't have the desired effect," the woman said, offering a smile. "Mind ya, we're going to give it a shot as well, just in case. Really, the important thing here is, no matter how you come to grips with it, you understand and accept your actions have consequences."

The woman dropped her cigarette on the floor and ground it beneath her heel before motioning to Skeeter. Kylie's breaths came in short gasps, and she struggled to calm herself as fear pulsed through her. Skeeter moved over to the railing and undid the knot. He pulled on the rope and lifted Kylie higher into the air. She bit her bottom lip, trying to hold back her screams. He secured the rope and stepped in front of her. The silence stretched out, and the woman cleared her throat.

"Well, go on now."

Skeeter let out a hoot and pulled a knife from the sheath on his belt. He waved it in front of Kylie, moving closer with each pass. She jerked back, and her body began to sway.

"My daughter accuses me of being too old-fashioned, but I'm a strong believer in right and wrong," the woman said with a shrug. "And when someone does something wrong, they must pay for that mistake. An eye for an eye, so to speak."

Kylie's gaze darted from the knife to the old woman, and she began to tremble.

"Pretty and smart, but don't worry, that's not your lesson today. I don't want to upset Jimbo any more than he'll already be," she said with a shake of her head before locking eyes with Kylie. "But your sister, on the other hand ..."

"NO!" Kylie shouted, her body twisting and turning while she struggled to get free.

"Maybe next time you'll think about it before going around all half-cocked. And don't you worry none, Mary Lou learned a whole bunch before they kicked her out of school," the woman said, motioning for Skeeter to take hold of her. "That said, we still need to get that spirit of yours under control. Skeeter's gonna help us with that."

He stepped forward and punched Kylie in the stomach, leaving her gasping for breath. He slipped the knife in her waistband and sliced down the hem of her sweats to her sneakers. He jerked her pants off and tossed them off to the side. He ran his fingertips over the front of her cotton panties and made a guttural sound deep in his throat.

"Now's not the time for your carnal pleasures," the woman said, her tone sharp. "Now's the time for teaching. Give her ten lashes, and if she fails to learn today's lesson or Jimbo grows tired of his new doll, we will revisit it."

Skeeter glared at Kylie but pulled his hand away. He slid the knife back into the sheath and pulled a leather strap from his back pocket. He unfolded it and moved to stand just behind her. She tried to look back, to see what he was doing, but her arms were in the way. She jerked when he snapped the leather strap against itself, the loud pop echoing through the barn. A giggle slipped out, and he did it again.

"Please don't do th—"

She hollered in surprised indignation as Skeeter slapped the leather band against her buttocks. She squirmed in the air and tried to swing away from him.

His laughter grew, and he struck her again, this time across the back of her legs. Her eyes bulged at the pain, and she began to wail. The woman motioned, and he smacked the strap against her bare skin again. Tears leaked from her eyes, and she dangled limply before him, unable to do much more than twitch at each strike as the pain overwhelmed her senses.

Skeeter moved closer and grabbed her hips, angling Kylie so she was between him and his momma. His tongue snaked out of his mouth, and he pressed the tip where her skin had broken open. He groaned, slipping his lips over the spot, and began to suck. Kylie whimpered but didn't try to pull away.

"Jesus Christ, that's enough, Skeeter," the woman barked. "Now get over here and help your sister. Jimbo'll be done feeding the dogs any minute."

He planted a kiss on her backside, smearing her blood on the ass of her white panties. "You taste so good," he mumbled against her back. "Don't you worry none. You and me … we're gonna have plenty of time to play."

8

Kylie struggled to focus through the agony. Pain pulsed through her legs and backside, and tears leaked down her face. The old woman was gone, and she watched as Mary Lou finished placing lid speculums in Sara's eyes across the room. She motioned to Skeeter for a scalpel and shifted until she blocked Kylie's view of her sister. Mary Lou motioned again and, after a few seconds, grabbed the forceps he held out. She shifted again, and bile rose up Kylie's throat as she watched her sister's eyeball get pulled out from the socket.

Kylie's stomach heaved, and vomit splashed across the floor.

"God damn it," Mary Lou barked. "You need to clean up that mess." She leaned forward and pulled the optic nerve taut. "But first, hand me those scissors." She snipped the eyeball free and dropped it into a container filled with a clear liquid solution. She screwed on a lid and placed it into a cooler.

"One down," she called out with an exaggerated sigh. She moved to the other eye and soon had it clamped securely in the forceps.

The door banged open, and Mary Lou jerked in surprise, ripping through the optic nerve and launching the eyeball across the room to land with a splat into Kylie's vomit. Jimbo pushed in the cart.

"God damn it, Jimbo," she barked, spinning around to search for the eyeball.

"What?' he asked, his eyes growing wide when his gaze fell on Kylie. "What is going on?"

Skeeter knelt and scooped up the vomit covered orb. "Found it."

Jimbo stomped toward Kylie, his hand shooting out when he stepped closer to Skeeter. He jammed his palm into the man's chest and shoved. "What did you do?" he howled.

Skeeter stumbled back, waving his arms to try and regain his balance. The eyeball squirted from his fingers and bounced on the ground once again. He grabbed the rope but slipped in Kylie's vomit and fell backwards. The sudden jerk pulled the knot free, and the rope went slack.

Kylie plummeted down to the floor and landed on Skeeter with a grunt. She felt something smoosh beneath her elbow, and rage swelled up in her chest. She started pummeling him with her fists, slamming them into his chest, stomach, and crotch. He hollered out in pain. Jimbo reached down to scoop her up and pulled her tight against his chest. Skeeter laid in a daze, clutching his groin and moaning softly.

A loud banging sounded from the tables. "God damn it!" Mary Lou screamed. "Get over here; she's coding."

Jimbo opened the stall and laid Kylie down on the hay. She curled into a ball and began to sob. Jimbo let out a shuddered breath and reached towards her.

"I need help, NOW!" Mary Lou screamed.

He jerked back and closed the stall door with a huff. The lock clicked in place. Kylie desperately wanted to cover her ears and block out the sound of Sara dying, but she was too afraid to move. Too afraid they'd discover she now held Skeeter's knife.

9

The barn had been quiet for hours, but Kylie still could hear her sister's screams. She wasn't sure what happened, none of her captors stopped to explain, but she knew her sister was dead. Allison sat beside her and stroked her hair while she cried, and after a few minutes, Ben crawled next to her and wiggled into her arms. She buried her face into his dirty brown hair and imagined she was holding Sara until the tears dried up.

"I can't stay here," she mumbled, sitting up. Ben clambered into Allison's lap and stared at Kylie with wide eyes. She shifted her leg and showed them

Skeeter's knife. "With this, we can all get out of here. I just need to open the lock. Are you with me?"

Allison grew still but, after a minute, nodded. "How?"

Before Kylie could answer, the outside door opened. She hurried to the wall and peeked through the cracks. Skeeter stumbled into the barn, holding a bottle of Captain Morgan's in one hand and a microwave burrito in the other. She scrambled back to the center of the pen.

"Hide in the corner," she hissed into Allison's ear. "Once he comes in here, I'll use the knife on him. Be ready to run."

Allison crawled back into the corner and pulled Ben into the shadows. Kylie lay back down, trying her best to position herself like she was when Jimbo dropped her. She could hear Skeeter shuffling around, pausing every now and then to drink. He banged his head against the stall and fumbled with the lock. The door swung open.

"I brought you something to eat," Skeeter said, his words slurring together. "To show you I have no hard feelings." He pulled off the bandage to reveal a bloodshot eye. "See? Not so bad."

He leaned over Kylie, and a splash of rum poured from the bottle and landed on the hay. "Whoopsie," he mumbled and slipped down to sit. He placed the bottle off to the side and held up the burrito. "It's big enough to share. I'll cut it in half."

His free hand slid across his waist, and he groped around the sheath. "That's weird … Where the hell is it?"

Kylie opened her eyes and sprang up, driving the knife into his side. She jerked the blade free, flinging blood across the stable wall before driving the blade back into his belly. Skeeter's eyes grew wide, and he dropped the burrito to press his hand against the wound.

"Hey, that's my knife," he murmured, swaying back and forth. The sticky red liquid pumped from the gash, soaking his hand in blood. His eye rolled back, and he tumbled over with a shudder.

Kylie scrambled to her feet and snatched up the bottle of rum. "Come on," she said, motioning to the open door. Allison started forward, but Ben stopped and stared down at Skeeter laying on blood-soaked hay.

"Come on, honey," Allison pleaded, pulling on his arm. He glanced up, his wide eyes shining with tears. "Baby, it's going to be okay. We're almost out of here."

Kylie bit back her snide comment and instead encouraged him to move. Allison pulled again, and this time he shuffled past the body. *Thank God.* Kylie left the thought unsaid and started to splash the rum across the walls and floor of the stable. She rushed over to the cabinet and started to dig around. She cried out in surprise and snatched up a key ring with three keys and a book of matches. Rushing back to the stall, she pulled a match free and lit the book on fire. Kylie held it for a moment, letting the flame grow.

"Get ready," she called out.

Allison herded Ben to the door and peeked outside. "Looks clear."

Kylie nodded and dropped the flaming book on the rum-soaked hay. A loud whoosh sounded, and the fire raced around the tiny enclosure. She turned and rushed to the exit. They stepped outside, and she closed the door. She guessed it was probably just after midnight, and she hoped that meant the rest of the family was asleep.

"If we're lucky, we'll be far enough away when they realize the barn is on fire," she said, holding up the key ring. "We just need to get back to the rest stop; these are my uncle's keys."

They crept down the line of the barn, staying in the shadows. She glanced up, grateful to see an almost full moon above. She prayed the clouds stayed away so they'd have a chance to make it back. Kylie

35

held up her hand and stopped. She glanced around, trying her best to get a lay of the land.

There was a ranch style house to the left of the barn and a wide strip of dirt between the two where the old pickup truck and the car were still parked. A tall fence with rows of barbed wire at the top surrounded both properties, with forest surrounding about three-fourths of that. There was a gate and, on the other side, a dirt road that disappeared into the trees.

"This way. I think there's another gate further down the line, and then we're home free."

Kylie took a deep breath and rushed across the moonlit road, then released it when she slipped into the shadows on the other side. Allison and Ben chased after her, and they slid to a stop next to her. She glanced back at the barn and saw smoke pouring out of the side of the building.

She turned to Allison and whispered through gritted teeth, "We have to hurry."

She turned her attention to the fence. It was mostly wood, but lines of barbed wire crisscrossed the frame, with three more rows running across the top. She hurried down the fence line, poking and prodding various points until a section shifted. She motioned for Allison to hurry.

"It's big enough for Ben to slip through," she said, pulling the wood to the side. "But we'll have to climb over. I think there's a tarp in the back of the pickup. We can toss it over the top wires."

Allison nodded and squatted in front of the boy. Kylie spun and hurried to the truck. She noticed the window was down and pulled the door open to see if she could find the keys. She checked the visor, under the seat, and in the glovebox with no success. She gave up, knowing full well that time was running out. The barn was clearly on fire now, and she knew it would be any moment before Jimbo and the rest of this fucked-up family poked their heads out. She moved to the bed of the truck and found the rolled-up tarp. Barking started to fill the night air. *Time's up.* She reached in and lifted the tarp out. The barking grew louder. She glanced over to the fence and saw Ben disappear to the other side.

Allison turned towards the barn, but her eyes were locked on something further away. She began to motion for Kylie to hurry. She took a step but hesitated when the barn door burst open. Skeeter ran out engulfed in flames. He spun in a circle, his arms waving like he was trying to put it out. He shrieked and splashed down into a large water trough. The fire went out with a loud hiss, and she gagged as the stench of burnt flesh filled her nostrils.

The barking grew louder. An unseen screen door banged open, and Allison screamed, the panic evident in her voice, "Hurry! For the love of God, hurry!"

"Momma, they're trying to get away," Jimbo called out, his voice thick with sleepy confusion. "And the barn's on fire."

Kylie ignored the flashes of pain she felt with each step and rushed back to the fence. She held out the tarp, and Allison grabbed the other end.

"On three," she barked. "One. Two. Three."

They tossed the tarp up and it folded over the top of the fence to trap the barbed wire. She prayed it stayed in place and began to climb. Allison followed her, and they slowly made their way up to the top. Something slammed into the fence with a yelp, shaking it. Kylie's hand came down on a barb, and she cried out in pain. She glanced down, and four large dogs were barking and clawing at the fence below.

"There on the fence," Jimbo called out. "Git 'em."

The dogs began to leap up the fence, their jaws snapping closed whenever they got close to the women's feet. Kylie got to the top and shifted the tarp so it would stay in place. Allison was frozen a foot or so away.

"Hurry," Kylie pleaded. "You can do it."

Allison locked eyes with her, and for a moment, she thought the woman was going to start climbing again, but the look of determination quickly turned to terror when one of the dogs snagged the back of her pants. As the dog fell, it began to shake its head back and forth and jerked Allison from the fence. Her scream cut short when she slammed into the ground and the air was driven from her lungs.

The pack was on her immediately, their jaws tearing into her clothes and skin. Her blood soaked into the ground around her as they ripped chunks of her flesh from her body and wolfed them down. She reached up towards Kylie, her eyes wide, but when she opened her mouth to cry for help, she only managed a gurgle as her blood poured out. A dog ripped her nose off before devouring her cheek.

A shotgun blast roared, and Kylie tumbled off the top of the fence to land with a grunt next to Ben. Tiny spots of pain dotted her chest and face, but she ignored them and pushed up to her knees. Ben threw his arms around her, and she struggled to stand with his added weight. The dogs growled and barked on the other side, and she tried to ignore the sounds of them tearing Allison apart. She turned towards Mary Lou's car, parked just off the dirt road, and shuffled forward.

10

Kylie sighed in relief when the car door opened. She slid in and helped Ben crawl over to the passenger's seat. She looked in the cup holder, then the glove box, and pulled down the visor. A set of keys slipped free and bounced off the steering wheel to land on the floorboard. *Oh, my God.* She leaned forward and grabbed the keys. She stared at them in her hand, wondering if she would be able to start the car, let alone drive it.

Bloody images of Johnny flashed through her head, and her hands began to shake. The accident hadn't been her fault, but that didn't matter. Not to her. His parents trusted her to keep him safe, and she failed. She flinched when Ben placed his hand on her arm. She glanced over at him and tried to smile. He watched her with wide eyes but remained quiet.

"It's like riding a bike," she said to him, inserting the key into the ignition and starting the car.

An explosion rattled the windows, and Ben threw his hands over his ears. She looked back and saw the barn was engulfed in flames. *Serves those bastards right*. She reached over and patted Ben's leg.

"It's going to be all right."

He leaned across the console and buried his face in her side. She shifted her body so she could wrap her arm around him. She worried that he hadn't asked about Allison yet, and she hoped once they escaped, he had family somewhere to help him. Her throat tightened, and she wondered how she was going to explain all this to her mother.

Worry about getting out of here first. She put the car in drive and jammed down the gas pedal. The car lurched forward, and she slammed on the brakes. Kylie swallowed, then took a deep breath, letting it out slowly. *Just like riding a bike*, she reminded herself. She pressed the gas again, this time trying to be smoother. She could hear the dogs barking, and she glanced at the rearview mirror. Her heart began to race, and her mouth grew dry.

"Oh no," she mumbled, her eyes glued to the larger gate swinging open.

Kylie tore her eyes from the mirror and pressed down on the gas. The car sped up, and she moved her hand from Ben to the steering wheel. She slid her hands to ten and two, just like she learned in Driver's Ed. The road swerved to the right, then left, and back to the right. She wanted to slow down, but she knew there was no time for caution. She tightened her grip and told Ben to fasten his seatbelt.

He burrowed tighter against her side, and she glanced down at him. "Please, Ben. You need to get back on your side and buckle up."

He shook his head, rubbing his face against her side and grunting what she thought could only be the word no. A loud roar sounded in the distance, and she knew she had no choice but to speed up. The road swerved back, and she jerked the wheel too far. The car began to shake as the tires hit the rough, uneven earth. She yanked it back the other way, and the car slipped from the road into a deep divot.

"God damn it!" she cried out, letting go of the wheel with her right hand so she could scoop under the boy and put him into the passenger's seat.

Ben squealed in frustration and pushed back harder. The car began to shake, and she struggled to control it. It popped free from the divot, and the wheel jerked out of her hand. The road curved back again, but they drove straight off it and began bouncing over the rocky ground. Screaming, she snatched at the

45

wheel. The headlights illuminated the first fence ahead, and she slammed on the brakes. The car shuddered but continued to race towards the wooden posts and barbed wire. She turned the wheel hard to the left, and the vehicle began to fishtail. She threw her body on top of Ben's right before the car slammed into one of the posts.

Every nerve in her body cried out from the sudden jolt, and she prayed she didn't pass out from the pain. After a few deep breaths, she forced herself to rise enough to check on Ben. He squirmed into her lap, and she hugged him tight. The rearview mirror caught the truck's headlights fast approaching, and she pushed the driver's door open.

Hurry, hurry, hurry. Kylie stumbled on her first step and almost dropped Ben. She shifted him in her arms and carried him to the fence. "I have to put you down so we can get through the fence. Then we need to go through the trees. But I promise once we get on the other side, I'll pick you back up. Okay?"

46

She waited for him to react, and after what seemed an eternity, he nodded. She put him on the ground and helped him wiggle through without any trouble. She stared at the wire, unsure if there was any spot she might be able to squeeze through. Kylie glanced back and saw the truck barreling closer. *No time*, she thought and squirmed between two rows of barbed wire.

Her shoulder instantly caught on one of the barbs, but she dug her fingers into the dirt and kept pushing with her feet. She yelped when her skin tore free, and she wriggled forward. She struggled to her feet on the other side of the fence and grabbed Ben. Kylie hugged him tight and began to shuffle towards the trees. The headlight grew brighter, and she wondered if he could see them. She picked up the pace.

Almost there, she repeated the two words in her head like a mantra, hoping to will them into existence. The truck's engine roared, and the headlights swept over them as the vehicle veered to the right and continued down the path towards the first gate. Kylie stood frozen for a second, convinced Jimbo saw them and was coming back. *Don't just stand there*, she screamed inside her head. *MOVE!*

Kylie stumbled forward into the forest. The trees were spaced out a bit and allowed the moonlight to filter down and light their way. She tried to keep up a steady pace, but even with the light, she found she had to slow a bit to work through the undergrowth. Her back ached, and each tortuous step sent a shockwave of agony through her hamstrings and buttocks.

Suddenly, she realized that the moon she thought she was staring at was actually a street light. A streetlight sitting on top of a hill. *We're almost there.* She sped up, desperate to escape the woods and get to the car. She kept churning her legs, straining to push through the suddenly thick underbrush that tore at her bare skin. She glanced back once again, curious why the dogs hadn't been sent. If Jimbo was out looking with the truck, why didn't they release the dogs as well? She flashed to the image of them tearing Allison apart

48

and wondered if that was the answer. Maybe they wanted to do something much worse to her for causing so much trouble. She didn't want to imagine what those maniacs might consider worse.

Lost in thought, Kylie didn't sense the shift in the ground, and she lost her balance and tumbled to her knees. Ben flew from her grasp and slammed into the ground with a grunt. He began to roll away from her, wailing for her help. He bounced once, twice, and then disappeared. A loud metallic snap echoed through the night, and his cry abruptly stopped.

Kylie scrambled forward, crawling down the incline until she came to a row of bushes. She could see where Ben had rolled through, and she pushed her way through. On the other side, her breath caught, and she struggled to comprehend what she was looking at. Ben lay caught in what looked like the jaws of a giant set of metal teeth. The spikes stuck through his face and neck, and blood gushed out of the wounds. Moonlight reflected off his unblinking eyes, and she reached over to swipe a stray strand of hair from his forehead.

The blare of a semitruck's horn pulled her attention forward, and she realized she was about two hundred yards from the edge of the rest stop. A sob caught in her throat, and she struggled with the idea of leaving him behind. She stood, and after another moment of staring down at his lifeless body, she crept forward. It wouldn't do to grow careless now.

Guilt washed over her. *No, you were careless enough with Ben, just like you were the last time you were behind the wheel.* The thought stabbed her in the chest, and she struggled to catch her breath. *Don't give up now.* She nodded, praying there would be help in the parking lot.

Kylie stopped at the edge of the woods and waited. There was some traffic noise coming from the highway, but nothing from the rest stop parking lot. She took a deep breath and stepped out onto the grass. She tried to stay in the shadows and hurried across the edge of the bottom of the hill until she worked her way to the front. A pair of headlights shined bright from the highway exit. It seemed far enough away, and she stepped into the artificial light and walked forward.

There was a sudden roar of acceleration from a vehicle approaching the rest stop from the exit ramp, and she realized it was Jimbo's truck. She ignored the pain in her legs and dashed towards her uncle's car. Pulling the keys out, she slid in front of the car and darted to the driver's side door. The truck pulled closer, and she struggled to keep her hand steady enough to insert the key. It scraped against the paint, once, twice, but the third time she slipped the key in and unlocked the door.

Kylie crawled into the front seat and ducked down as the truck's headlights illuminated the interior of the car. She clenched her eyes closed. The truck rumbled past, and after a few minutes, she opened her eyes and sat up. She glanced to the left and saw the taillights glow red, and then the truck turned right and disappeared into the woods. She slipped the key into the ignition and bit her bottom lip. Should she start the car? Could she? She sat there wondering, when a throat cleared from the backseat.

Kylie's eyes darted to the rearview mirror, and she watched Mary Lou lean forward and jab a needle into her neck.

"Where do you think you're going? We still need those eyes."

END

There's Something In The Water
Expanded Edition

All Kurt Reedy needed for his lakeside development project to go through was the land owned by Chuck Miller. The only problem was Miller refused to sell his family's legacy. In the past, Reedy may have resorted to violence to get his way, but he was a legit businessman now.

Running out of time, he is forced to think outside the box. In his haste, he doesn't do the proper research, and now there's something in the water.

Something territorial.

Something hungry.

53

THE SURROGATE

In their search for a surrogate, the Wilkenses thought they struck gold with Alina. All she wanted was a flight to the United States and a warm place to stay during the pregnancy.

But some things are too good to be true ...

Kiss Me Where It Smells Funny

Alex has a crush on the new Teacher's assistant, and he's finally worked up the nerve to approach her.

Too bad she's crossed the University's star player, and Duncan Shaw has no choice but to make her disappear.

He plans to lay the blame on the local urban legend, but tonight he just might learn that some legends are real.

THE DONN, TX COLLECTION
VOLUME 1
IN PAPERBACK

There's a place in Texas the locals avoid, where the lost go missing and the damned reside. You won't find it on any map, there are no road signs to guide you, and if you have the misfortune of finding it, may God have mercy on your soul.

Run, run as far as you can, for when The Scarecrow wakes, the harvest of blood begins.

Welcome to Donn, TX.

Gateway to Hell.

1969, 1865, 1926

And the short story that started it all:

Donn, TX 1952

Individual years are available on ebook & Audiobook.

DONN, TX 2002

Patrick Smite is now following in his father's footsteps as the sheriff of Donn, TX. His sister, Laura, is worried he won't be able to do all the job requires. For while he believes he can keep the town safe, she knows the awful truth: they must honor the family's obligation to The Pale Man, no matter the cost.

Danielle Kipler is on the run. The Pale Man in her dreams promised her sanctuary. The only thing required is her undying allegiance. But is she prepared to make the necessary sacrifices to become a citizen of Donn, TX?

Years ago, a pact was made that requires payment in blood. For in the end, all that matters is the harvest.

DONN, TX 1978

Sheriff Harold Smite has done all he can to make the yearly harvest run smoothly, but something out in the corn is dying to get free.

Jane Lipman faced the harvest nine years ago and survived. She's done everything she can to make peace with the past, but Donn, TX isn't done with her.

Bonnie Smite thought she was simply run down, but she's been chosen for something special. Something only The Pale Man knows about and he's not sharing.

Welcome to Donn, TX: Gateway to Hell.

THE POPE LICK MASSACRE

There are two types of people in Jefferson County: those who know the legend of the Pope Lick Monster and those who believe it. Before the night is over, Sam will have no choice but to join the believers.

Since their mother's death, Sam's sole focus has been taking care of her younger brother, Kenny. Now Kenny's Scout troop is missing, having never returned from the woods around Pope Lick. Sam gathers a group of friends to search for the boys and their Scoutmaster. With each step, they get closer to discovering the scouts aren't the only ones in the woods this night.

The Ephraim Godwin Chronicles
The Sins of the Past

Once an ancient race of supreme beings ruled over the earth. Banished by the light centuries ago, one has returned. With the help of its disciples, it desires to plunge the world into a new age of darkness and horror.

Ephraim Godwin is searching for the truth about his family's disappearance. After conventional ways failed, he turned to the world of spiritualism, only to discover it filled with charlatans and tricksters. As a known skeptic, Ephraim fights to shine a light on those who prey upon others as he searches for the truth.

As Ephraim attends another séance, he discovers not everyone is a fraud and is drawn deeper into the world of the supernatural. With the help of noted spiritualist Zona Whitlock and famed explorer Doctor Livingstone, he hopes to stop this evil from consuming the world.

ABOUT THE AUTHOR

I'm an indie Horror writer who lives deep in the heart of Texas. When I'm not writing novels and stories for anthologies, I'm doing the bidding of two adorable huskies. I've been married for over twenty years and have a teenager in the house, so I won't be running out of horror material for quite some time.

Enter a world of horror …

Printed in Great Britain
by Amazon